Merry Christmas, Everybody!

By
Constance
Allen

Illustrated
by
David
Prebenna

A
Random House
Pictureback®
Shape Book

CTW Books

Copyright © 1993 Children's Television Workshop (CTW). Sesame Street Muppets © 1993 The Jim Henson Company. All rights reserved under International and Pan-American Copyright Conventions. Published in the United States by Random House, Inc., New York, and simultaneously in Canada by Random House of Canada Limited, Toronto, in conjunction with Children's Television Workshop. Sesame Street, the Sesame Street sign, and CTW Books are trademarks and service marks of Children's Television Workshop. Originally published by Golden Books Publishing Company, Inc., in 1993. First Random House edition, 1999. Library of Congress Catalog Card Number: 99-60884   ISBN: 0-375-80370-X
www.randomhouse.com/kids   www.sesamestreet.com
Printed in the United States of America   10 9 8 7 6 5 4 3 2 1
PICTUREBACK, RANDOM HOUSE, and the Random House colophon are registered trademarks of Random House, Inc.

On the day before Christmas, Grover was in a very big hurry.

"Merry Christmas, everybody!" he called as he rushed down Sesame Street. "I do not have time to stop right now because tomorrow is Christmas!"

"Merry Christmas, Grover!" called the Count. "Look at all the beautiful snowflakes! Do you want to count them with us?"

"I would love to," said Grover. "But I am a very busy monster today."

"Hello, Grover!" called Elmo. "Elmo and Rosita are making snow angels. Do you want to make one, too?"

"Not right now!" answered Grover.
"I have something very important to do."

"Oh, look!" said Grover. "Here is Nickles Department Store. I have to stop in here for a moment."

"Pardon me. Excuse me. Clear the way, please."

"Merry Christmas, Mr. Santa Claus, sir," said Grover. "I would like a red fire truck, please. I have been a very well-behaved little monster. Thank you very much, and now I really must be going."

"Oops! So *very* sorry, sir. Let me help you
pick up these packages. Merry Christmas, sir!"

"Yoo-hoo, Grover!" called Cookie Monster.
"Do you want a Christmas cookie?"
"No time for cookies now, thank you," said Grover.

"Merry Christmas, Grover!" called Snuffy.
"Do you want to ice-skate with Alice and me?"
"I cannot stop now!" answered Grover.

"Hey, Grover!" called Merry Monster.
"Want to help us decorate the Christmas tree?
Oscar helped make the ornaments."

"And I get to put the star on top when we're all finished!" said Big Bird.

"Thank you, everybody, but I am in a terrific rush!" said Grover, and he dashed away.

"Jingle bells, jingle bells,
Jingle all the way.
Oh, what fun it is to ride
In a one-horse open sleigh!"

"Merry Christmas, Grover!" called Bert.
"Want to come Christmas caroling with us?"
"Thank you, but I must be dashing through the snow," answered Grover as he ran.

"Merry Christmas, Grover!" said Telly. "Look at the wrapping paper we made in play group. Isn't it neat? Want to come wrap presents with me?"

"Thank you, Telly, but there is no time to lose!" called Grover. "Clear the way, please!"

"Oh, joy! Here I am at last!" said Grover when he got to the post office. "I hope my cousin Fred will receive this present in time for Christmas."

Grover hurried up to the counter and said to the clerk, "Do you want to know what I am sending to my cousin who lives in Florida? If I tell you, will you promise not to tell him?"

"I am sending him…"

"SNOWBALLS!"